# Adventures With Blaze

# The Rescue

**Author:   L. Wayne**

**Published by   L. Wayne**

**Copyright © 2017   L. Wayne**

A fictional account of how three teenagers spent an exciting summer of their 15th year.

Mystery, betrayal, fear, excitement and worry awaited this young trio.

The saving of a colt and the capture of a thief.

ISBN-13  978-1976381522
ISBN-10  1976381525

# Dedication

I happily dedicate this book to all youngsters who love and dream of horses.

# TABLE OF CONTENTS

# Adventures With
# Blaze
# The Rescue

**CHAPTER 1**

Slowly walking toward the lot where his dad had parked, Buck begin to think about what he might do this summer, now that school was almost out. His 15th birthday was coming up, and the summer held a lot of promise. *Fifteen in a month. I can hardly wait,* Buck thought.

*Buck pondered the fact that none of his friends called him "JJ" any longer. It was that one time when ol' Peanuts threw me to the ground,* Buck recalled, *that was when the nickname stuck.*

It was a couple years ago when he, Scotty and a few friends were at the corral on dad's ranch, the Bar W. Someone in the group dared JJ to ride the old roan horse called Peanuts. Peanuts got her name because she seemed a little nutty at times, and had this skittish streak.

JJ could not let the dare go unchallenged, so, he threw a saddle and bridle on Peanuts and climbed

1

aboard. Instantly, Peanuts went into a crow hop and dropped her head, as if to start bucking. JJ yanked back on the reins to get her head up, but he knew he was in trouble when Peanuts ears went back, and she started prancing sideways. Her moves were fast, and JJ quickly found himself hanging on, feet firmly planted in the stirrups, and hands grasping the saddle horn. At the same time this old tom turkey, while strutting around the place, jumped on the fence and gave out a loud gobble gobble. Ol' Peanuts jumped sideways and back on her hind legs, and before JJ knew what was happening, he found himself flying off and landing on his backside in a fresh pile of ol' Peanut's poop.

Well, to JJ's friends that was great entertainment. Scotty, his best friend, said, "Hey Buck! *Good* job. You showed that old horse who was boss." They were all applauding JJ, and giving him 'high fives.' "Hey Buck," Scotty teased. "Our favorite cowboy who can't stay on a horse." So, from then on JJ's name became J.J. "Buck" Winslow. JJ really didn't mind, in fact, he rather liked his nickname.

"Hey Buck," JJ's friend Scotty called out, interrupting Bucks thoughts. "What's up for the weekend?"

"Not much Scott, but I suppose dad has a few chores for me." Buck responded. "If I can get away from the ranch I might go and see if there's any fish in the ol' fishing hole."

"How about me tagging along." Scott replied. "If we catch anything we can tell lies about it just like all us *expert* fishermen do." Scott laughed.

"Great, call me tomorrow and we'll make some plans. You always had your way around the truth." Chuckled Buck.

While climbing into his dad's car, Buck spotted, out of the corner of his eye, the new girl in his class. Her name was Katherine, but her new friends called her Kate. She had long brown hair pulled up in a ponytail. Buck caught her eye and shyly smiled. She waved and said, "Hi." Buck waved back, and climbed into his dad's car.

"Who was that young girl?" Dad ask.

"She's new in school," Buck replied. "Her parents moved here from someplace back in Missouri. Her dad trains horses, and figured his opportunities were better out here."

3

They had driven for a few minutes when dad turned to Buck and said, "I have a few things for you to do this weekend. Your mom and I are going to a livestock sale down by Donley. We're going to see what kind of livestock is available on the market, and to check the local prices. We will be back in a couple of days. Big Ed will be at the ranch looking after things, if necessary. You're getting old enough so you can begin taking more of the responsibilities upon yourself. I want you to keep your eye on the cattle. I am reasonably sure that they should be okay."

"There has been a wild wolf spotted in this part of the county, so I want you to keep an eye on the livestock. I'm not too concerned, but just in case check the herd occasionally." Dad continued, "I would like for you to check the pond on the east section, too see how much water it has. If there is very little, we will need to move the herd closer to the big pond, which has plenty of water. That should keep you busy."

"Dad, Scotty and I would like to go fishing." Buck said. "We could do the job together. The cattle are close to the river and we could stop for a while and try our luck."

"That's fine, but don't neglect your

responsibilities." Dad replied.

"One other thing," dad said, "Joe Tanner is coming over this weekend to tend to ol' Sparky. Sparky's hooves have been sore lately, and he will probably need to re-shoe the old horse. Stay close while Joe is here, and watch him work. You might learn a few things from him."

After supper that night, Buck went to bed early thinking of what he would do this weekend. *Scotty and I could saddle up a couple of the horses and do our chores. We could take our fishing poles with us, and find a quiet place to fish.* Before his eyes got too heavy, he thought of that new girl in school, Kate. He smiled and immediately fell asleep.

# CHAPTER 2

The next morning Bucks dad called out, "Get up Buck! Time for breakfast. Your mom and I are going to be leaving in a little while."

Buck turned over and moaned about having to get up so early on the weekend. He stretched and thought of going fishing with Scotty, and immediately bounced out of bed with an eager desire to start the day.

At breakfast, Mom asked, "JJ, what are you planning on doing today?"

"I have some chores to do for dad and then Scotty and I are going fishing a little later." Buck replied.

Dad looked at "Buck" and said, "JJ, don't forget what I asked you to do. It's important for you to look after the cattle and check the water in the pond."

"Okay dad." Buck responded.

Buck finished breakfast, and headed for the barn to tend to his horse, Jasper. Buck was not sure how Jasper got his name but it seemed to suit the animal. Buck fed Jasper some hay and topped it off with a scoop of grain, to get the horse ready for a day in the saddle. Jasper flicked his tail back and forth, dislodging a couple of horse flies and seemed to enjoy the extra treat.

"JJ, you have a phone call." Mom called.

Buck hurried to the house, knowing it was Scotty.

"Hey Scotty," Buck breathlessly spoke into the phone, "what's up?"

"Are we on for fishing today?" Scotty asked.

"Yep," Buck answered, "Mom and dad are going to Donley for a couple of days. I have some chores to do, but we can get in a little fishing, as well. So, why don't you come on over. We can get our stuff together, and get started."

"Be there in half hour." Scotty shouted excitedly.

Buck had already picked out a horse for Scotty to ride; Ol' Thunder was one of the cattle ponies - well trained and eager to go. They saddled ol' Thunder, for Scotty, and prepared to be on their way.

"Let's double check to make sure we have all our

fishing gear with us, and we can't forget a snack for lunch." Scotty said. "Don't forget your .22 rifle, we might be able to get in a little target practice today."

As the boys hurried about getting their gear in order, Buck heard a car in the driveway. Buck thought, *I wonder who that might be, this early. Oh yes,* he remembered, *Mr. Tanner is coming over to shoe one of the horses. Dad wants me to stick around while he's here.* Buck looked at his watch and thought. *I didn't know he would be here this early.*

Buck thought about what he should do. He was aware of his dad's wishes, that he be here. In the middle of his thoughts a car door slammed, and he heard a couple of voices he didn't recognize.

Big Ed, the ranch foreman, called out from inside the barn, "Is that you Mr. Tanner?"

"Yes, Big Ed, we're here," Mr. Tanner called out.

When Big Ed walked out of the barn, Mr. Tanner was leaning against the corral fence. Mr. Tanner was a rather large man, and standing beside him was another man and a young girl about Buck and Scotty's age. Buck smiled when he recognized

Kate, the new girl in his class, at school.

"Hey Buck, come over here," Big Ed called. "I want you to meet someone." Buck and Scotty walked out to the corral, and while glancing at Kate, said, "Hi Mr. Tanner."

Mr. Tanner said, "This is my friend Chuck Samuels and his daughter Kate." Buck stuck out his hand, shook Mr. Samuels's hand, and nodded to Kate. Buck had no idea that he would see Kate so soon again.

"Big Ed, Chuck is new in this area and is starting a business, training horses. His daughter Kate is an accomplished rider, for her age." Mr. Tanner said, motioning toward Kate. "When she knew we were coming here, she wanted to come. Hope that's alright with you."

"Of course," Big Ed said. "How about you Buck?"

"That's just fine, but Scotty and I are going back into the field to check on some cattle and a pond on the east section. After that, we are planning to do some fishing. Our day is filled and we won't be back until late this afternoon."

"That's okay," Kate said. "I'll just stick around here until Mr. Tanner and dad are finished."

Buck turned to Kate and said, "There's one thing, your dad said you were pretty good with horses, and if that's true you could come with us, if you want." Buck offered.

Kate's eyes lit up and with a big smile on her face, said, "Yeah, I would like that."

## CHAPTER 3

About half an hour later, the boys had gathered a few more supplies, and another lunch mom had made for Kate.

Buck and Scotty took Kate into the corral and ask, "Do you want us to pick out a horse for you or do you want to do it yourself?"

Scotty smiled under his breath and said, "This one here is old and very gentle and would suit a girl of your expertise."

"How about that black spotted one standing by the fence," Kate replied.

Buck winked at Scotty and snickering said, "That's Cracker, we used to call him firecracker but shortened it to just Cracker. Whoever rode that horse, after they were thrown off, they'd exclaimed 'he's a real *firecracker*'."

"I'll take him," Kate sweetly smiled.

With everything ready, they climbed on their horses, and headed out.

They were a happy trio off for a day of

exploration, and adventure.

"Hey Buck, what do we do first?" Scotty asked.

"I think we should check on the cattle first. It'll take about an hour."

They rode the well-beaten trail for about 30 minutes when Buck said, "Why don't we go over by the river, and see if we can find the fishing hole where dad and I caught that 15 pound flathead."

"Great Idea, let's do it," responded Scotty. "Is that Okay with you, Miss Kate?"

"Yes, and don't treat me like a helpless girl. I'll race you to the river and the last one there has to take care of my horse when we get back." She playfully replied.

Buck looked at Scotty with this sly grin on his face and said, "Okay, it's a race." Off they went at a breakneck, hooves flying, run. Buck was experienced as a rider and Scotty was a fair one, but when they saw Kate staying with them they knew they might have misjudged this girl, and made a mistake in agreeing to her challenge.

They urged their horses faster but Kate stayed with

them. After about a half-mile run they came to the river and Kate was right with them. They slowed down as they approached the river, and found a place to stop where they could water the horses. Sliding out of their saddles, they walked over to an area where the water was shallow, but very swift. Buck picked up a rock and skipped it across the river and as he did, he noticed what appeared to be a very large dog watching. "Did you see that Scotty?"

"No, what did you see."

"I am not sure but it looked like a large dog. It wasn't a dog that I recognized." Buck said, wondering.

"Kate, did you see it?" Buck asked.

"I just got a glimpse of it," Kate said. "I don't think I have ever seen a dog that looked like that. It looked mean."

After watering the horses, the three of them were a little spooked and concerned. They mounted their horses, and headed toward the herd.

Buck was the first to break the silence. "The reason we are going to check the cattle is because dad said there was a wild wolf roaming around this area."

They rode on for a while thinking about what they had seen and a little concerned about how many of those animals might be out there. If they saw one there could be more.

About a half hour later, they came to the pasture where the cattle were grazing. They stopped on a ridge, where they could see the entire herd. The herd, grazing peacefully enough, seemingly were unaware of their presence.

The three of them watched for a while and decided to ride down to the herd to have a closer look. Upon reaching the cattle, everything appeared peaceful, so as a final check they circled the cattle, and inspected them for any signs of trouble.

"I believe they're all okay, I don't see any signs of distress. I am still concerned about that wolf we ran into back there." Buck said.

"Hey Buck, how far is the pond we have to inspect?" Kate asked.

"About half a mile to the North. Just over that rise and just past that grove of trees." Buck replied.

"Why don't we stop at the trees and have a little lunch and rest the horses? After all, they must be tired after Kate ran them so hard." Scotty said teasing Kate. We can let her unsaddle our horses and let her fix our lunch." Scotty boldly kidded.

Buck looked over at Kate, and saw fire in her eyes and a little smirk on her face.

"Okay, I'll do that just for you guys, just because you are starting to act a little strange. We see a wolf and you go funny." She smirked again, and said to herself. *Just wait.*

They reached the trees, found an area with grass enough for the horses, and decided this was where they would rest. After climbing off their horses, Buck and Scotty handed the reins to Kate. Kate had this look in her eyes that the boys did not recognize. She took the reins and led the horses off a little way and before the boys knew what she was doing, she climbed back on her horse and started around the trees toward the river, just over the hill.

"Hey Buck, what's she up to?" Scotty shouted, looking toward Kate as she rode off. "Hey Kate, where are you going?"

"I am just going to water the horses and take care of them, like you said I should." She gently responded.

"Come back, you have our lunch," Scotty yelled.

"Oh, that's right, if you want to eat you can follow me to the river. I'll water the horses and if you're there in time we can eat." Kate said, looking over her shoulder.

"Do you think that she'll come back?" Scotty asked Buck, a little afraid he might not get lunch.

"Well, you know, I think she might be a little prankster. She must have been planning this after we teased her about the horses." Buck responded.

Kate stopped the horses about 20 yards away and turned around to the two boys. "Okay, I'll tell you what I'll do. You take care of your own stuff and I will take care of mine. 'Promise?' If you don't you can find your horses in the barn. Still saddled."

"Okay! Okay!" Buck and Scotty shouted in unison. "Come on back and we'll stop acting like jerks."

"Okay," Kate said. And as she came back, she handed Buck and Scotty the reins of each of their horses, smiled very sweetly, and said, "Here you are guys." She turned around, so they could not see her face, and almost laughed out loud. This was a story to tell the girls at school; how she outsmarted the two big shots.

# CHAPTER 4

"She sure got us on that one." Buck chuckled. "We must watch her very closely, she may be smarter than we gave her credit for," Buck laughed.

"Yeah, we can get back at her if we try," Scotty whispered.

Kate grinned as she sat down on a nearby log and opened up her lunch sack. "You clever guys just try." she teased, for she had overheard Scotty's whisper.

After a few more jabs at one another, all the while laughing at each other's quick wit, they decided to get back on the path to the pond.

Buck sprang into the saddle, with Scotty and Kate following. As the three left the camp, they began to see just how beautiful the area was, the landscape, the rolling hills, the wildflowers and the grove of trees. They reflected on the fact that it was a very beautiful area of the ranch. Buck said, "Someday, I am planning to build my house here in this beautiful location," They fell silent as they continued riding toward the crest of the hill.

"Buck, what was that?" Kate anxiously asked

hearing something she didn't recognize. "It sounded awful.

"I heard it, and it didn't sound very good." Scotty replied. "It sounded as if one of the horses may be in trouble. Maybe we better get over this hill and find out."

They pushed their horses into a canter, and as they came to the top of the rise, they were astonished to see before them a horse in big trouble. A snarling wolf was attacking the animal. The wolf was making a lunge at the mare, while biting, snarling and inflicting injury to the horse's legs.

"Buck, we must do something, that beast is hurting the horse." Kate yelled.

Buck remembered his .22 rifle he had brought along, and reached for it.

The mare was beginning to show that she was exhausted. She stumbled a few times, and under the severe onslaught, finally collapsed. The wolf seeing its chance attacked the horse with a wicked vengeance and tried to finish the fight.

By this time, Buck had the .22 out, aimed it at the wolf, and fired. The distance was greater than the range of the gun, but the shot caused this vicious predator to pause in its attack.

Buck knew he had to get closer to the horse if he was going to save her. He kicked Peanuts in the flank and off they went at a hard run toward the injured animal. When Buck got closer, the wolf's attention became riveted on Buck and the other riders.

Buck paused and fired another shot at the ferocious animal, this time taking careful aim. He was gratified with hearing a yelp from the wolf, and watched as the creature ran toward a clump of trees, about 100 yards away.

The three rode up to the mare and soon began to see that she was badly injured, and totally exhausted from her ordeal.

Kate was the first to speak. "What are we going to do, Buck?"

Buck began to feverishly examine the mare, and knew very quickly that she was in terrible trouble.

"Scotty, you and Kate go back to the ranch as quickly as you can, and bring Big Ed. Tell him what happened, and to bring Mr. Tanner and

Kate's Father with him. I don't know if we can save this horse, but we have to try."

Scotty and Kate turned their horses toward the ranch, and raced with all the speed that their animals could muster. The ranch was some distance away, and they knew it was a race against time.

Buck, in the meantime, was trying to help the animal as best he could. There didn't seem to be much of anything he could do but comfort the horse and wait. He had his rifle, and his main goal was to keep "that mangy wolf" away from the mare.

The horse, laying on its side, tried to raise its head and gave out a weak cry while Buck continued to stroke, and comfort the animal.

After a few minutes, the mare became quiet. Buck, thinking maybe she had just gone to sleep, didn't grasp that the mare had just died.

Buck stood and looked around for the wolf, and was surprised to see the wolf edging toward the pond. Buck quickly grabbed his .22 from the saddle scabbard. After taking careful aim, he took a shot at the wolf. The wolf yelped, but this time the wolf did not run. He continued to stalk something in the pond. Buck was not able to see the near side of the pond because of a shallow rise. He decided to have a look, while keeping the rifle in his hand, ready for anything from the wolf.

When Buck reached the small rise, he was startled to see about 30 feet out in the pond a young horse of about 2-3 weeks old. The little animal was thrashing around in the water, scared and calling intermittently for its mother. The wolf was crouched, intently watching the young animal. His attention was so riveted on the colt that it had not yet detected that Buck was very close. The wolf continued to inch its way to the edge of the pond, while keeping its evil eyes focused on its prey.

Buck yelled at the wolf, the wolf turned toward him and let out a snarl, with its teeth bared, while backing off just a bit.

Buck knew he must help the colt, who was thrashing about in a state of panic, trying to protect itself from this savage animal.

Without thinking the matter through, and with his desire to help this helpless little animal, Buck leaped to his feet and ran into the water toward the colt. Not realizing the wolf was eyeing him, Buck was not sure what he should do, but realized that he had just committed himself.

Buck knew he had a couple more bullets in the gun and thought he could keep the animal away or with a lucky shot maybe even kill it.

Buck got to the colt; put his arms around the little feller's neck to stabilize it in the water, and to help ease its anxiety. Buck began to grasp that he was in deep trouble, with a skittish little horse and a raging wolf.

Buck began to be aware that the only thing he could do was to wait out the wolf, and hope that help would come soon. He also knew that it was going to be at least half an hour before help arrived, so he uneasily settled down to wait.

## CHAPTER 5

The wolf moved back a short distance from the pond, and looked around, seemingly losing interest. As things got a little less tense, Buck relaxed a little, and figured he might be able to lead the colt out of the water. As they moved slowly toward the bank the wolf got up from its resting place and began to walk toward the water's edge, once again. Buck decided to use one of his two last bullets and try to get a good shot at the beast. As he raised the gun, the wolf snarled and growled causing the colt to panic. The startled colt jumped up on its hind legs, knocking the rifle from Bucks hand.

*What am I going to do without my gun?* Buck thought. *If I go down in the water to retrieve it, the wolf might see its chance to attack. If I don't go down, will I be able to frighten the wolf away? Maybe.*

Again, the wolf saw its chance and made a lunge toward the little horse, going into the water about five feet. The water was deep enough that the wolf instinctively knew that he would be at a disadvantage if he were to fight in water almost as high as his head. He knew he had to wait them out.

Again, the beast retreated, but also seemed to know he was not in any danger, at the moment.

Buck held on to the young animal while soothing it, but both were getting very tired. Buck was deeply concerned that if help didn't come very soon they would be too tired and cold to stay in the pond. The bottom was soft mud, and very difficult to move about in. Buck, feeling concern for his safety and the safety of the little horse, knew he must wait out the return of Scotty and Kate. Shivering, Buck mumbled to himself, "where are they, it has been 30 minutes since they left?"

Hoping that they would hurry, Buck did not know that he was going to have to wait out in this cold pond much longer than he expected.

**

Scotty was ahead of Kate when they started for the ranch, but Kate quickly overtook him. She was going flat out at a full gallop, wanting to get help as quickly as possible. It seemed the ranch was a million miles away, even at a full out run. It was only a run of a few minutes, but it seemed to take forever.

Dashing into the barnyard, Scotty and Kate began shouting for Big Ed. When the men heard the commotion, they came running out to see what was causing all the racket. Big Ed, upon seeing the two without Buck, became fearful that something dreadful had happened.

Scotty was first off his horse, almost before it came to a complete stop, and Kate slid from her saddle, stumbled in her haste and regained her footing.

Speaking fast and out of breath, she tried to explain the problem. Scotty filled in the areas that Kate had left out and between them; they were able to relate the story.

"A wolf had attacked a mare and the horse was seriously hurt. Buck had stayed back there to protect the horse. Buck had his rifle and the wolf was probably wounded although we don't know how badly."

"We'll take the pickup," Big Ed shouted.

The three men set about getting the pickup out of the shed and getting down to the pond as quickly as possible. Big Ed, disgusted with himself, remembered the last time he drove the pickup the battery was dead. His intention of replacing the battery was forgotten because of another pressing matter. He climbed into the pickup hoping the truck would start, but it didn't.

"We need to change the battery, the truck won't start," Big Ed cried out.

"Let's take my car," Mr. Tanner quickly volunteered.

"I don't think your car can make it through the runoff area, with those deeply rutted tracks. The truck can make it; we'll just have to replace the battery." Big Ed replied. "Mr. Tanner, you remove the old battery while I go into the tool room and fetch a new one. We must hurry," replied Big Ed.

**

*I wonder how much longer it will be before they get here with help.* Buck thought. *I am getting tired and cold, and this little guy is giving me fits with its fighting the water, and me.*

The wolf was pacing up and down the bank of the pond snarling, and glaring at Buck and the colt. Stopping occasionally to get a drink of water, the wolf continued to pace.

The wolf seemed to sense that it was going to have to move soon or leave to find another prey, which would be much easier to catch. He continued to watch and wait for the right opportunity to do his dirty work.

The colt continued to thrash about, tossing Buck from side to side. The colt suddenly tossed up its head and hit Buck in the face. Buck suddenly found himself in the water, completely submerged. It happened so fast that Buck had no time to react. Buck groped for footing, in the soft bottom. Finally, his hand found a large branch, which had fallen from a nearby tree. Grasping the branch, he immediately came to the surface only to find the colt in a state of panic, and the wolf, now in the water, creeping toward them.

## CHAPTER 6

Buck, with his heart pounding fiercely, did not know what he should do. The only thing he could think of was to raise the branch over his head, in a threatening manner, and shout and yell at the top of his lungs.

The mangy wolf stopped its slow pacing, and raised its filthy head to see Buck waving a weapon. Backing into the shallow water, the wolf squatted down, and seemed to attempt to figure out the problem.

The colt began to calm down, giving Buck a chance to rest a little from this ordeal. Buck was becoming extremely exhausted, and very cold. The colt was beginning to settle down a little, and Buck, becoming a little more confident, again stumbled in the soft mud but this time he didn't go under. He regained his footing, and began to realize that they were at a stalemate. The wolf on one side, and Buck and the colt on the other. The question in Bucks mind was, *who could outlast the other.* Buck knew he had been in the cold water for some time and it would not be possible to last much longer. *"Would they get her fast enough,"* He thought.

**

When Big Ed returned with the battery, Mr. Tanner still had not removed the old battery. The bolts holding the battery cables were very rusty and corroded. They were almost impossible to disconnect. Big Ed ran back to the shed for some rust remover and after squirting some on the nuts and bolts, they finally came loose. The battery was changed, and a few minutes later they were racing toward the old pond.

Big Ed was driving, Scotty and Kate were in the cab while Mr. Tanner and Kate's dad were in the back.

They arrived in a cloud of dust, as Big Ed brought the truck to a shuddering stop.

"I see the horse over there, but where's Buck?" Kate cried out. "I don't see him."

"Let's fan out and see if we can find him." Big Ed said, taking charge.

The men, fearing the worst, said nothing to Scotty and Kate for fear of frightening them.

Kate heard something and as she turned her head toward the pond, she heard it again. "I think I hear

30

him over by the pond," she yelled.

When Kate topped the small rise, she was able to see what was happening, and her heart went cold; Out in the pond was Buck holding this little horse and a vicious wolf snarling at them.

Kate gasped at what she saw, and cried out, "Big Ed, there, in the pond, and a vicious wolf is after them!" She shouted, pointing.

Big Ed joined Kate, and immediately told Mr. Tanner to get the rifle from the truck, and shoot the wolf. *Big Ed's rifle was much more powerful than Buck's .22.*

Kate shouted to Buck, "Were here Buck! Mr. Tanner is going to shoot the wolf. We'll get to you and the colt in just a minute."

**

Buck heard the truck arrive, and as Big Ed jumped from the pickup, he turned to Mr. Tanner and say something Buck wasn't able to understand. Then the most welcome sound Buck had heard in a while, "We're here Buck. Mr. Tanner is going to shoot the wolf. We'll get to you and the colt in just a minute." Kate shouted.

With all the confusion, the wolf bolted toward the clump of trees, but when Mr. Tanner fired the wolf tumbled and rolled, squarely hit by the large round from the rifle. The wolf lay very still, never again to wander the prairie. The ordeal with the wolf was over. A cold, hungry and tired Buck walked out of the water, his arms around the colt's neck to keep it from running away.

"I need a rope to secure this little guy." An exhausted Buck sighed.

Kate returned to the truck for a rope, brought it to him, and looking a little closer at the colt, said. "That is a beautiful little horse Buck. Look at the markings on its head. It looks like a blaze." She remarked, with excitement and amazement.

The little animal shook its head, placed its nose in Bucks chest and gave a little shove, as if to say thanks. At that moment, Buck knew he had a lifelong friend.

# CHAPTER 7

After the excitement had settled down, they got the colt into the back of the pickup and headed back to the barn. Buck, Kate as well as Scotty were in the back with the colt, while Mr. Tanner rode in the cab with Big Ed. All were in a good mood knowing that they had saved a young colt from disaster.

Chuck Samuels, Kate's father, volunteered to ride the horse Buck had ridden that day. As he rode back to the barn, he reflected on what had just happened, and was very thankful for the outcome.

Buck was the big hero of the day. He was happy and hungry, but still cold. He forgot those things for a while as he hugged the colt and grinned at the others.

"I'll take the backhoe and go out to the pasture and bury the horse and the wolf," Big Ed said. "I'll put the wolf in the hole as well. We don't want to attract any more wild animals."

In the meantime, Buck and the others unloaded the colt and took him into the barn. "He must be hungry and exhausted," exclaimed Kate. "How will we feed it?"

"I don't know," Buck replied. "Maybe we can get a milk bottle and fix a nipple to it. We have plenty of milk cows around so milk isn't a problem."

"You know, they make nipples for young orphaned calves," Scotty exclaimed

"That's right, and I know where they are," Buck exclaimed. "Mom nursed a calf last spring and left them in the feed shed."

While Buck went looking for the feeding bottle, Kate and Scotty found an empty stall, and some dry hay for the colt. They made a straw bed for Blaze to lay on, and placed a water bucket in the stall, as well.

When Buck returned with the nipple, they had the stall ready and the colt was already feeling at home in this warm and dry place.

"Great," exclaimed Buck, "I'll go get some milk and we will feed this little boy."

**

Kate was right about his markings, and the name "Blaze" was perfect. It stuck. Little did they know just how much interest this horse would spark and how great the name would become. Life with Blaze was destined to be rewarding, exciting and lively!

A few days later, Mr. Tanner and Chuck Samuels, Kate's father, walked in to see the young colt, and Chuck said, "Buck, I think this animal has a lot of potential. His lines are perfect. The shape of his head shows a spirit that only comes in a few animals of this caliber. This young animal has an excellent bloodline, and when he has grown, the sky's the limit. Train it properly and you will be amazed at the results."

As they walked back to the car, Mr. Tanner turned to Chuck and remarked, "This has been a great few days. We saved a young colt and killed a predator. The old mare is a shame, but she gave her life protecting her young. A good end for the old horse."

*

A journey of adventure begins for this trio of happy teenagers, in the summer of their 15<sup>th</sup> year.

## CHAPTER 8

Over the next few weeks the young animal grew at a rapid pace, and thrived at the attention it received from this lively trio of 15 year olds. They were with "Blaze" every day, and trained it as well as they knew how. Of course, Kate's father was a trainer of horses, and Kate continually ask him some very important questions about training, and then explained to Buck and Scotty what her father had advised.

One day the three were together at the ranch and Kate asked Buck, "Have you had him out in the field yet?"

"Not yet." Buck replied.

"Let's do it then. We can saddle our horses, put a halter on Blaze and take him out," Scotty shouted with eagerness.

They saddled up, placed a halter on Blaze, and headed out into the pasture. Blaze, not being used to being led around attached to a tether, at first resisted, but it didn't take him long to get used to the new experience. Off they went laughing, talking and teasing one another, expecting this to be a full fun day.

"Let's give little "Blaze" some training." Kate said.

"What do you suggest for the first lesson?" Buck responded, not knowing what they should do first.

"Well maybe we should work on calling him and for him to quickly respond to our call," Kate replied. "I remember dad said it's important for us to come when called and I think that Blaze should also come when called."

"How are we going to that?" Scotty asked. "That sounds like a difficult job."

"Buck, do you have a long rope?" Kate asked. "We'll need it to tether the colt and to give him some space to respond."

"How's that going to work?" Buck asked.

"Well, what we'll do is take Blaze out to the end of the rope and then call him and pull him toward us after we call him. The thing we need to figure out is what call sign or signal to give him so he will respond."

"How about, *Blaze here Blaze*." Scotty smirked.

"I think that's too long, and silly," Kate laughed. "You're not being serious." She scolded. "How about a whistle. We can whistle a note and when Blaze hears the whistle he will know it's us."

"Great idea," Buck exclaimed. "Not only will he recognize the sound of the whistle, the sound will carry much further than a voice command. With his sensitive ears, he will be able to hear the whistle from faraway,"

Buck quickly returned to the barn, found a couple of extra ropes, and tied them together. With the ropes attached, they secured one end to Blaze's halter. Scotty took Blaze out to the end of the rope and when he reached the full length, he turned Blaze toward the others and announced, "We're ready."

Buck knew the whistle he would use. Tongue in teeth with lips puckered, he gave out a loud attention-getting signal.

Blaze jumped when he heard the loud noise and pulled away. Buck and Kate firmly pulled the colt toward them. When Blaze got to them, Kate pulled a carrot from her pocket and gave Blaze the treat.

"You're very crafty, Katie Samuels. You knew what we were going to do today." Buck chuckled.

"It's about time you knew how smart I am," Kate grinned. "Oh, by the way, dad said that giving a treat works very well. You Buck, don't get a treat for you don't work very well." Kate laughed.

So the three spent the next hour taking Blaze out to the end of the rope and then whistling and pulling him in. After about an hour, Buck asked if Kate thought they could take the rope off and see what Blaze would do. They agreed to try it and see what would happen. Immediately, when they released Blaze from his tether he jumped, turned and with head held high and mane flying, ran at breakneck speed toward the north pasture.

"Well, that worked well," Scotty exclaimed. "Where do you think he's going?"

"Well, let's follow and find out." Buck replied.

Mounting up, they followed the young animal. They were amazed at how fast this little horse could run. He was galloping with a full stride and moving very quickly. After reaching the crest of the small hill Blaze came to a halt, and just stood there.

"Wonder what he's doing?" A confused Kate whispered. "He's just standing there."

Buck whistled to call Blaze, and was astonished to see him turn and come back to the three of them. Kate took out another carrot and gave it to the colt.

"I don't understand, what just happened?" Kate asked. Blaze nuzzled Kate's hand, turned and trotted back the way he had come.

"Let's see where he is going," Buck said.

They followed the Colt up the small rise, where Blaze again stopped. Apparently, he was looking out over the pasture.

"Will you look at that," Scotty exclaimed. "That's the pond where you rescued him, and over there is where Big Ed buried his mother. Do you reckon he's aware of all that."

Still pondering the actions of this young horse, they decided to head back to the barn. Buck whistled and Blaze trotted along behind, as this happy trio walked their horses back toward the corral. Not saying much while lost in thought,

Buck began to see that they had a great little horse and it *seemed* a very smart one, as well.

Blaze, being a quick learner, picked up commands very easily. He was a happy little horse, and the three were extremely happy with how Blaze was developing. Over the next few weeks this happy trio devoted a great deal of time to this little horses training, while their attachment to him became very strong.

## CHAPTER 9

Late in the summer, Buck and his parents were sitting at the breakfast table. Buck was munching on pancakes, when dad said. "Buck, did you know that Wilson County is having a Labor Day parade? The school is organizing a display, and a float, to be designed and built by the students, for the festivities. They would like the students to display some of their summer projects, and give a demonstration or set out a display. I was thinking that maybe you, along with Kate and Scotty, would be interested?"

"Yes, I would," Buck replied. "We have been working with Blaze all summer, and I think he would do very well. He is only about 5 months old now, but he is coming along nicely. Kate's dad says he has a lot of potential."

"You only have two weeks to get him ready," Dad remarked. "Can you do it?"

"You bet!" Buck exclaimed. "I'll call Scotty and Kate. I know they will want to be a part of this."

For the next couple of weeks the three pals worked together with Blaze. Kate taught the colt to rear up on its hind legs and to throw its mane. Scotty and

Buck were continuing to work with him, to follow without a tether. They worked hard training Blaze, so that the young horse could show its true and full potential.

One evening at supper, dad remarked to Buck's mother, "Lee, have you noticed how much these kids have done with that colt? It's nothing short of amazing what they have accomplished in such a short time. I believe they have a very good chance of winning the blue ribbon, as best of show."

Buck's mom replied, in a low voice. "I hope you're right, I know they would be so disappointed if they lost. That is such a nice little horse."

*

The day of the parade had finally arrived, while firmly securing Blaze in the horse trailer, dad turned to Buck and asked, "Did you know that the O'Donnell's have an entry in the parade. They are having a display and demonstration after the parade. Their son has been working with a young filly, and I hear that they are bringing their best to the competition."

"I haven't seen Jimmy all summer, and didn't know he had a project, let alone a young horse. I'll be curious to see him and his horse." Buck replied. "I don't think his horse stands a chance against Blaze," Buck continued. Although this was the first time that Blaze had been out in public, a concerned Buck said to himself. *We can't lose, Blaze will make us proud.*

*

When dad pulled into the parking lot, Buck spotted Kate right away, waved her over and said, "Did you know that Jimmy O'Donnell has an entry in the parade."

Kate looked at Buck with a surprised look on her face, "No, I didn't," she replied

"It's a young filly that he's been training and working with all summer. It's about the same age as Blaze."

"Well, Mr. Buck, I think we will win so don't get so worried," Kate scolded. "By the way, where's Scotty. He's supposed to meet us here."

**

Scotty's dad had parked in the other lot, about forty yards from where Buck's dad had parked, so Scotty had a little time to walk around the enclosures where the displays and animals were

44

being kept. While walking, he spotted a familiar face, walked over and said, "Hey Jimmy, what's up?"

Jimmy turned and saw Scotty, waved and grinned while saying, "Hey Scotty, what are you up to? Staying out of trouble?"

"Well, I am here with Buck and Kate Samuels to show off our summer project."

"Yeah, me too," Jimmy replied. "I've been working with this young filly all summer, and I think she's ready to show."

"Well, I've been working with Kate and Buck this summer, but they are too hard to train, so we are training a young horse we rescued." Scotty laughed. "We've been working with Blaze all summer, and we are putting him in the parade and the display afterward."

"I bet he can't beat my little filly." Jimmy chided.

"Let's have a look at your little girl, and see if I agree." Scotty cautiously laughed.

Jimmy motioned with his hand, "Come on back and see our famous little filly known as Princess."

45

The boys sauntered back to see the filly. Jimmy proudly pointed out the little horse, and said. "There she is Scott, the horse that will give your Blaze a run for its money." Jimmy chuckled proudly.

To Scotty's amazement, she was a beautiful colt with a mostly black coat and white stockings. Her freshly combed mane was gently blowing in the soft breeze.

"She's a beautiful horse," Scotty exclaimed. "She'll have a hard time beating Blaze though. Have you seen Blaze yet?" Scotty asked.

"No I haven't," answered Jimmy, "Let's go and see this *famous* horse of yours."

Off they went to where Buck and Kate were tending to Blaze. Looking sideways at Kate, Jimmy said. "So, *this* is the famous Kate with a horse called Blaze, I have been hearing about." chided Jimmy.

"Jimmy O'Donnell what are *you* doing here?" Kate bristled. She knew Jimmy because he sat behind her in class, and at times, he could be a real pest. Teasing her, and making a pest out of himself.

"I've come to see the great Blaze, and to tell you that Princess will beat you in the judging." Jimmy boasted.

"No she won't," Kate objected. "You just watch and see, Mr. Smarty pants."

Jimmy grinned at Kate and said, "We'll see Katie," as he walked off. Jimmy put on a good show but he was concerned. He had never seen a colt like Blaze, and it began to sink in that he had some tough competition on his hands. While returning to his little filly, his mind went back to Kate, he smiled to himself and thought, *yes, she is very pretty.*

## CHAPTER 10

Over the loudspeaker came the notice to line up and "Let's get the parade started!" The rush to get in line was a little confusing at first, but order was quickly restored, because all entrants had been assigned a position. The High School marching band began to play, and to lead the festive parade. Behind the band came the cheerleaders and behind them came the sports teams. With cheers and shouts, the crowd loved it.

The band played the school song, the cheerleaders jumped and did cartwheels, and with their pom poms in hand, they put on a great show for the town folks. The sports teams came next, behind them came the floats, and behind the floats came the farmers and their displays. Some showed bushels of corn, others displayed vegetables. One farmer had brought twin calves. The 4H had their displays as well. It was a cheerful occasion with everyone in a great festive mood.

The parade organizers knew that the livestock should come last for obvious reasons. You didn't want the band and cheerleaders dodging horse manure.

The parade organizers had placed Jimmy's little

filly and Blaze side by side, thinking it would not interfere with either horse, for the streets were wide and there was plenty of room. One of the main judges had another reason, because he wanted to see the two colts side by side. It would make judging them much easier.

As they marched closer to the stands, Buck removed the leash from Blaze's halter, and gave him the signal to stop, and stop he did. Kate and Scotty stopped with Blaze, while Buck continued to move forward. When the parade began getting closer to Blaze, Buck whistled, and Blaze threw his head up, and with mane and tail flying, raced to Buck. The crowd cheered. Buck then raised his hand, and gave a command; Blaze rose on his hind legs and pranced a little for the crowd. The crowd roared its approval.

Jimmy was amazed at what Blaze had done, but he had his own tricks to do. Jimmy whistled, and Jimmy's dog rushed out of the sidelines, and jumped on the little filly's back, all the while turning in circles. As the filly rose on her hind legs the dog jumped off, and with a stroke of Jimmy's hand, the little filly bowed to the crowd. Jimmy grinned with delight, raised his hand and took a bow.

"He's *such* a show off," Kate grumbled to Buck and Scotty. "We are still going to win the overall award."

The parade finally ended, and the displays judged. The 4H exhibit won an award, the farming community also won many awards, but the final award was the best of show for the animals.

The judge rose to the platform, and with a blue ribbon in his hand, said. "We have a decision to make about this award. As you know, the two participants in this competition, the young filly of Jimmy O'Donnell and the young colt of JJ "Buck" Winslow, are fine young animals, who both demonstrate excellence in training. They have made it difficult to choose one over the other. The judge paused, "*This* decision has not been an easy one."

Buck looked over at Jimmy and he had a smile on his face, although Buck thought he seemed rather worried. Buck smiled back, and raised his thumb up for Jimmy to see, but he was worried as well.

The judge continued, "When we see fine young animals trained by these *talented* young people, our hearts are warmed for the future of this community. We have been fair or to the best of our ability to be fair, so knowing you want me to shut up and introduce to you the winner. (The crowd chuckled) I will *proudly* do so."

"The winner is Blaze and his trainers Buck, Kate and Scotty."

The crowd roared its approval!

After the noise of the crowd subsided, the Judge said. "Jimmy O'Donnell should not be disappointed because he has done an *excellent* job with his filly and he is awarded the red ribbon! The ribbon says second place, but with all of the people in this crowd Jimmy is a winner as well."

The crowd went wild again and there were many happy faces. Buck, Kate and Scotty gave high fives to each other, raced over to Jimmy, and shook his hand.

The day was a big success, and the three teenagers were happily looking toward the weeks to come.

# CHAPTER 11

Big Ed, while walking towards his pickup, was pondering about the day's events. The day's activities had settled down, and people were in the process of packing up to return home, "Hey, Big Ed!" a voice called from his left, interrupting his thoughts. "Haven't seen you in a long time."

Big Ed turned toward the voice, and to his surprise stood a person he had met a few years earlier, while he was in the county jail. He had spent six months in the county lock-up for a very foolish act of breaking and entering. It was a time in Big Ed's life that he was not proud.

"Well, what do you know, it's old Sam from my days of crime," Big Ed retorted.

They shook hands, and Sam said, "Why don't I buy you a cup of coffee or a soft drink, being they don't have anything harder at this here shindig."

"Why not," Big Ed replied, as they turned toward the refreshment tent.

"What have you been up to these past few years, and are you staying out of jail?" Big Ed laughed. "You'll have to tell me all about what line of work you are in, and what's keeping you out of the big house." Big Ed chuckled.

"Well, Big Ed, I've been working for a carnival over in Masonville. My job is to scout new locations, and that is the purpose for me to be here in this little burg. Part of my job is to find horses that are trainable, and colts that could be trained for the circus life."

"Interesting," Big Ed responded.

"The colts need to be at least 6 months old so we can get them ready for a future in the circus ring. There are many thing that these horses can be trained to do, Big Ed. Let's just say, they need to be a smart, and a good looking beast." Sam explained.

"Why are you here in this area, Sam?" Big Ed asked. "This town's not big enough for a circus."

"Primarily, I am looking for horses to add to our stock. I happened to notice the colt that came from your ranch," Sam replied. "Do you think they would sell the animal for a decent price?"

Big Ed laughed, and said, "Are you *kidding*? You couldn't buy that colt for any amount. JJ rescued that colt with his two friends, and they are dead set on training him. The animal has a lot of potential and I believe they can, and will, continue his training. As you saw from today's events, they have already accomplished an amazing amount.

Sam thought about what Big Ed had just said, and he began to consider ways he might be able to get Blaze. If he could get the horse for the circus there would be a big bonus for him. A bonus that would put him on easy street for a while. Sam decided to think about how he might accomplish his newfound goal, of getting this young horse.

Ed interrupted Sam's devious thoughts, and asked, "Where are you staying, while in town?"

"I have a horse trailer on the back of my pickup, and it has a small sleeping area in the front. You understand, kind of like a home away from home." Sam chuckled.

Ed smiled, and said, "Why don't you come out to the ranch for a couple of days. I could show you around, and let you see what the kids have done with Blaze."

With a devious gleam in his eye, Sam said, "Great, I would love to come out and see the place. It's been a long time since I've spent much time on a ranch. It would remind me of the good times from my checkered past." Sam laughed.

Big Ed held out his hand, and they shook. "Nice to see you again, Sam. Just follow me to the ranch and we'll tell tall stories about how we saved the world, and what we have accomplished. If that doesn't work we'll tell lies to one another." They both laughed.

## CHAPTER 12

While riding back to the ranch, Buck thought of the day's events, and wondered just how far their colt would go. Blaze was smart, and full of energy and life. Buck dreamed of parades, where Blaze was the leading horse, with him in the saddle, all dressed out in western wear.

"Buck," Dad said. Waking Buck out of his daydream, "Did you see the fellow that Big Ed was talking to? They seemed friendly. I guess he was one of Big Ed's friends?" Dad questioned.

"Sorry dad, I didn't see him."

They arrived at the ranch, and set about the chores of getting Blaze out of the trailer and into the barn. Blaze was given some hay, and an extra measure of grain to finish off his triumphant day. Afterward, leading Blaze into the corral, to roll in the dirt, only then did Buck and his dad unhitch the trailer and park it. Father and son then set about doing their evening chores.

Big Ed drove up in his pickup, and upon climbing down, called out to Buck, "Hey Buck, nice show today, Blaze did a great job showing off his skills. You kids did a real nice job of training him."

About that time a pickup, with a horse trailer hitched to the back, pulled into the driveway and honked the horn.

"Oh *yeah*, Buck, tell your dad that I invited an old friend over and he will be staying for a couple of days, until his business is finished." Big Ed explained. "No worries though, he has his trailer and a cot in it for overnight. Come on over and I will introduce you to him."

Buck's dad heard the exchange, and came over to Big Ed with a puzzled look on his face. "You brought a friend back from the fair to stay for a couple of days?" Buck's dad asked.

"I hope you don't mind, if you do, I'll ask him to spend the night someplace else."

"No, that's fine. There is plenty of room. Just tell him to park out of the main drive and to make himself comfortable."

"Hey Sam, park that rig and come here. I want you to meet the Boss and his son, Buck." Big Ed shouted.

Sam parked the pickup, and as he climbed from the cab, he took one long look in the truck just to make sure nothing was there that might cause some suspicion from casual lookers.

Big Ed said, "Hey Boss, this here is my old friend Sam. We met a few years ago, and haven't seen much of one another for quite a spell."

Sam stuck out his hand, and dad shook it, "Thanks for allowing me to camp here for a couple of days," Sam said.

"Nice to meet you Mr. Winslow, you too Buck. That was quite a show you put on today. I would like to congratulate you on such a nice looking horse, and one that has the making of a very *fine* animal."

Dad Winslow was pleased with the stranger's compliments, but a little taken aback by Sam's demeanor. Dad was a little suspicious of Sam, but had nothing to go on but an uneasy feeling in his stomach. He thought about it for a moment, and decided to dismiss the feeling as nothing but old anxieties from his past.

"Big Ed will show you around, Sam," Dad remarked as he walked off. "Enjoy your stay."

Sam looked at Big Ed, grinned, and said, "I *surely*

will, Mr. Winslow."

## CHAPTER 13

Thanksgiving was just a couple of weeks away, and the ranch began to get ready for the winter months ahead. Fall was progressing nicely, with the trees turning their different shades of reds, orange and yellows.

Blaze was permitted to go into the pasture more often, now that he was about 7 months old. He was a very frisky, and energetic young pony. Rearing on hind legs and whinnying, and with mane and tail flying, he would run like the wind. He would roll in the dust and then shake himself. He enjoyed his life and he had everything a young horse could want. This ranch was home, and he was thankful, as much as he could be, being that he was a horse.

School had started a few weeks earlier, leaving little free time. While the three teenagers became more involved in their schoolwork, they could not spend as much time with Blaze as they would have liked. Buck and Scotty were involved in sports, and Kate tried out for the cheerleading squad. School was a busy time. Buck's parents attended a few county fairs around the area, looking for machinery and livestock for the ranch.

Big Ed was busy with his duties, repairing the barn and stalls, so that during the heavy snow and cold winter months, the barn would be warm for the horses. The hay, in the upstairs loft, mostly used during the past few months, needed to be restocked. There seemed to be an untold number of chores to be done.

As the weeks rolled on toward Thanksgiving, the only time, it seemed, for the three to get together and do anything with Blaze was on the weekends. The summer had been a great time for them, and their training of Blaze was very rewarding. Kate's dad helped them by giving instruction on how to go about the training, and setting up a plan for the future training of this very special animal.

**

"Hey Buck," Scotty called out. "Why don't we get together and do something this weekend, and take a break from school?"

"Great Idea," Buck answered. "We could get an early start and maybe hunt and fish for a spell. I was talking to Kate, in class this afternoon, and she mentioned coming out to see Blaze, and maybe doing some work on his training."

"We could do that this weekend. If we started by 8 Saturday morning we could work with Blaze and after that we could have the day free for some goofing around," Scotty offered.

Plans were made for Saturday morning, when all would gather at the ranch for the kind of breakfast that only Buck's mom could make.

**

It was just past midnight on Friday night, when a truck, with a horse trailer hitched to it, slowly moved down the road. The truck was dark in color, and with the lights off was very difficult to see. On this deserted farm road, the truck edged closer to the Winslow Ranch, and stopped about a quarter mile from the driveway. The driver of this rig slowly climbed out of the truck and adjusted his hat and dark coat. He put on his gloves, and slowly and quietly moved toward the driveway to the ranch. He was aware that the dog would start barking, but he figured, because he had met and befriended the dog a few weeks earlier, that the dog would recognize him and not put up too much of a racket.

The man stopped, and rehearsed his plan, then slowly and carefully, while sticking to the shadows, began making his way toward the barn.

There was a row of trees between the road and the barn, so his cover appeared to be okay, and would probably be enough.

There was a light on the exterior of the barn, illuminating the area around the barnyard. The stealthy thief thought he could go around the back of the barn, and slip in the back way, where the light cast shadows. Just to be sure, he brought with him a BB pistol, to shoot out the light, if need be.

Slowly, he crept toward the barn, and about halfway there, the dog began barking. The man paused, for a time, to let the dog settle down. When the dogs barking did not let up, he became puzzled as to why the dog didn't come over to him. He heard a shout from one of the windows for the dog to quiet down, and the barking stopped. *"Probably on a rope,"* he thought.

The man had about 60 feet to go before getting to the barn, and as he crept closer, he began to wonder if Big Ed were asleep. His cabin was just 50 yards behind the barn, and the barn was visible from his back window. If there was no light on in the cabin then Big Ed was probably asleep. He remembered from the past that Big Ed was a sound sleeper, and it took quite a commotion to wake him up.

The man slowly crept around the barn to look in the direction of Big Ed's cabin, and saw that the lights were out. He breathed a sigh of relief, and reached for the barn door.

He felt around for the slide bolt, very quietly slid it to the left, and opened the door a crack. He began to slowly open the door, because he did not want the hinges to squeak or to make any unnecessary noise. Sam slipped inside the barn, and very slowly and quietly, he closed the door. He began to look for the stall that Blaze occupied. The first three stalls were occupied. Making his way down the aisle, separating the row of stalls, he looked over the rail in the last stall on the right, and there was Blaze, looking at him, with wide eyes.

Blaze seemed to know that something was not right, and moved backward into his stall. The man slowly opened the door, and slid into the stall. Sam carried with him a black cloth that he had made for this occasion: - a hood for Blaze's head, a covering for his eyes, which would keep the horse from becoming too frightened by the strange things happening.

With a smooth voice and outstretched hand, the man touched the horse's bridle, and with a slow movement placed the cloth over Blaze's eyes and secured the covering with a couple of bungees going under the throat of the puzzled animal.

The man slowly reached out, snapped a rope to Blaze's halter, and begin to lead him from the barn. Once at the door, the thief paused to look around and make sure that all was safe and no one was awake. Big Ed's cabin was still dark, and he guessed that the dog was in the house. The way seemed to be clear. Slowly, they began to walk back toward the road, where the truck and trailer were waiting. The rustler knew he needed to hurry as much as possible but not to be in such a hurry as to make a disturbance. It took about ten minutes before they reached the trailer. Slowly and quietly, the man opened the tailgate. There was no noise, because the man had freshly oiled the hinges. Slowly and carefully, he worked.

He took Blaze to the front of the trailer and tied him into the stall (he had the foresight to put some hay in the stall). The thief had also padded the stall, because he didn't want the horse to injure itself in this rough riding trailer, and it would provide some soundproofing, as well.

Sam quietly closed the tailgate, locked it, and climbed into the pickup. Slowly, he drove down the road for a couple of miles and finally, breathing out a sigh of relief, turned on his headlights and entered the highway, heading south.

**

Sixty miles south, the truck and rig were traveling well within the speed limit. To attract attention from the State Police would very likely put an end to this caper, and land him back in jail. Sam smiled to himself, and thought, *how easy it was to get the horse.* Of course, *they were nice people, the Winslow's, but a little sloppy in not locking the barn door.*

*We'll get some distance away as fast as possible and we'll take the horse to old Jerome, my favorite horse thief and trainer,* He chuckled to himself. *He knows good horseflesh and if I cut him in on the deal, we can sell this little critter for a bundle.*

Sometime later, in the distance Sam spotted his turnoff. He slowed down, allowing the oncoming traffic to pass, before he started his turn. He knew his old former friend and buddy, Jerome, was about two miles down this road, and then a long driveway back toward his house and pasture.

Sam crossed the old bridge, found his turn, well hidden among the trees. Turning right, he began to follow a strange and foreboding tree-lined lane. Sam thought to himself, *this place is spooky. I wonder how he will treat this horse. He's a little spooky himself.*

# CHAPTER 14

Bucks mom fixed a great breakfast, because she knew that this was going to be a busy day for these kids. Pancakes, eggs, with some bacon and hash browns. Fresh orange juice and milk, for dunking her homemade chocolate chip cookies. Mom and dad were cheerful, because they could see the kids were excited about today's venture.

"Great breakfast, Mrs. Winslow, you always know how to put on a feast." Scotty exclaimed. Kate nodded her head in agreement and said, "Thanks for everything." Buck, while pulling on his sweater said, "Let's *go*, we have things to do today."

"Have we got everything Buck?" Scotty wondered aloud. "Yep, I checked this morning and we're all set." Buck responded.

"I stuck a couple of your mom's cookies in my pocket, just in case I get cookie withdrawal." Laughed Scotty.

The trio set out for the barn with high expectations, discussing the day ahead. A wonderful day with Blaze and a full day of goofing around. Eagerly discussing what to do first, they quickly closed the distance to the barn. Kate reached the barn door first, swung it open, and stepped into the darkened structure. The door was closed, so she knew Big Ed was not in the barn.

"Big Ed's not here," she exclaimed. "Maybe he slept late this morning, and will come over a little later."

"Doesn't matter," retorted Buck. "We can saddle our own horses, and be out of here in a few minutes."

In the first stalls, the horses were contentedly munching and eating their hay, but the back stall door was open. "That's strange," exclaimed Buck. "Maybe Big Ed didn't secure the stall last night."

Kate walked back to the stall to see Blaze, and when she looked into the stall, the colt was not there.

"What happened to Blaze?" she cried out. "He's not here!"

Both boys ran to the back stall and looked in, thinking that Kate was trying to have a little fun with them. When they peered into the darkened stall, there was no horse.

"Where do you think he is?" Scotty asked. "Do you think that Big Ed was here, and took Blaze out for some reason?"

"Big Ed's cabin is out behind the barn. Let's go and find out," Kate said, "Buck, I don't like this,"

So, off they ran toward Big Ed's cabin. When they arrived, Big Ed opened the door, and said, "Sorry, I overslept this morning."

"Have you seen Blaze?" they all cried out in unison. "He's not in his stall. The stall door was open and Blaze is gone!"

Big Ed looked at each one of them and seeing the frightened look on their faces, realized that they were not kidding.

"Blaze is missing," cried Kate. "How could he have escaped from the barn? Both doors were closed. Only the door to his stall was open."

They looked at one another, and Scotty, in a worried voice, ask, "You don't think that Blaze could have been stolen, do you?"

Buck and Kate turned to Scotty, with mounting fear in their eyes, and immediately looked at Big Ed for an answer.

"I don't know." Big Ed responded. "It's a possibility, Buck. Let's go see your dad, and see if he has any answers."

They ran off toward the house, with Big Ed bringing up the rear.

When they rounded the side of the barn, Buck saw his dad close to the corral, getting ready for his morning chores.

"Dad!" Buck called anxiously, "Have you seen Blaze?"

Dad stopped, and looked at the panicked group. Shaking his head, he said, "No, I haven't seen Blaze since about dark last night. I believe Big Ed was the last to see him."

They all stopped, with concern and fear beginning to rise in their thoughts. Kate burst out saying, "Blaze has been stolen!" The others looked at her in disbelief, but knowing deep down that she was probably right.

71

Dad looked at Big Ed, and told him to saddle one of the horses, and start looking around the pasture and the surrounding area for any sign.

Scotty asked, "Can I go with Big Ed?"

"Yes," Dad responded. "That will give you something to do while we call the Sheriff and get him out here."

"I'll go with Scotty and Big Ed," announced Kate. "With the three of us we can fan out and cover more area."

"Buck, you go into the house and ask your Mom to call the Sheriff. We going to need him out here as quickly as possible. The longer we delay, the further away the thief could be."

# CHAPTER 15

The three rider's rode around the barn looking for clues, but didn't see anything promising.

"Scotty, you go out into the north pasture and see if Blaze might be there, and Kate, why don't you go toward the pond, and see if Blaze might have gone back to the area where he was born. I'll look around here for a little longer, and then look to the south." Big Ed instructed.

Meanwhile, Buck's mother phoned the Sheriff, and Buck decided he would wait out by the fence for the Sheriff to arrive. As Buck leaned against the fence, he began to think about the past few days, and what the little horse meant to him. He had a hard time holding back the tears. He knew he must do something, while he waited for the Sheriff.

Buck, while walking back toward the barn, glanced down at the driveway and saw a faint hoof print, and next to the hoof print, he saw the print of a boot.

Buck stopped in his tracks, being very careful not to disturb the dust around these prints. He began to look more closely, and realized they were the prints of a man leading a horse. He began to consider the ranch activities, and knew there were no horses in this area yesterday. His only conclusion was that they were the tracks of the person who had taken Blaze.

Very carefully, he followed the tracks out to the road, and then followed them up the road a couple hundred feet. The tracks of the person, and the horse, ended in a set of tire tracks. The tire tracks were large, and could only belong on a trailer. Buck knew at once how Blaze had been stolen. His heart sank into disbelief, knowing that to get Blaze back would require a great deal of work, and a good amount of luck.

*Where to start,* Buck pondered. *I know very little about detective work, and I am not sure just how much time the Sheriff will give to finding Blaze. He is a busy man, so I guess the job is on the three of us.*

**

Kate, riding slowly, and looking for any signs of Blaze, wondered just where the colt could be, and if he were in any danger. The wolf that had killed his mother might have had others that he ran with, which could cause him harm. The worry she had for his safety, was almost overwhelming.

As she rode on, the thoughts in her mind turned to the time when they had rescued the little colt, and had taken such a desire to protect the animal, and to give it a good life. She remembered how Blaze had been easy to train, and how he had won at the fair some weeks before. There were many memories flooding through her mind, as she looked carefully for Blaze or any tracks that she might recognize as belonging to Blaze. As she reached the pond, her thoughts returned to that day when she saw Buck and Blaze in the pond being stalked by the wolf. She smiled at the thought that they saved the little creature, and that he had become an important part of their life. Remembering these happy times, she sadly rode on.

## CHAPTER 16

Big Ed sat on his horse, trying to understand what had happened, and how it could have come about. How *had* the colt gotten out of the barn? The door was closed and latched, which meant that someone had gotten into the barn, and led Blaze out. They then closed and secured the door, so no one would suspect anything, unless they were entering the barn, allowing him extra time for getting away.

Did he know *anyone* who would do such a thing? If he did, *who* could it be? His mind was racing, trying to think if he might know anyone who might do such a thing as steal a horse right out from under his nose.

Big Ed thought about Sam, whom he had recently encountered at the fair. *Would Sam actually do something that deceitful?* After thinking about the matter for some time, he discarded the idea that Sam could have stolen the horse. He had known Sam for many years, and because of their friendship, he *surely* would not do such a shameful thing. The answer must lie somewhere else.

Big Ed continued to ride, and with a heavy heart continued to look for Blaze. He knew that rustlers were not kind people, and hoped that whoever had stolen Blaze had a kind streak, and would cause him no harm.

**

Scotty saw Kate and Big Ed in the distance, and quickly caught up to them, asking. "See anything? I saw nothing of Blaze." He continued.

"No, we came up empty," Big Ed exclaimed. "Let's get back to the barn and see if the Sheriff is there yet."

As they rode into the corral area, Scotty spotted Buck standing in the road with the Sheriff. They appeared to be talking excitedly. After dismounting, and leaving their horses in the corral, they rushed over to where Buck and the Sheriff were standing. The Sheriff was quietly talking to Buck, while pointing down at the road.

As they walked up, the Sheriff said, "Watch where you step. We have some footprints and tire tracks. It appears that whoever took your horse loaded him into a trailer and hauled him away. You people stay here for a while, I think I will drive down to the main highway, and see if I can get the direction they turned."

**

Arriving at the highway, the Sheriff got out of his patrol car, and very carefully looked for tracks that might tell him which way the vehicle and trailer had gone. There had not been much traffic on the road this morning, and he very quickly spotted the tracks. The tracks were going south. *What is south of here?* The Sheriff thought. *I sure hope they didn't take the horse across the border into Mexico.*

After returning to the ranch the Sheriff said, "Well, it appears that they have gone south. I am not sure where they could have gone, heading in that direction. There is nothing south of here except a few farms, and Donley. Donley is not a big enough city to sell a horse like Blaze. He will be famous in a few days, with this crime being in the papers, and I doubt seriously that a rustler would take such a chance."

The Sheriff asked a few more questions, and wrote down the important information needed about Blaze, his markings and his height. "I'll place this information in the computer and see if anything turns up," he said. "It will go out later this morning and hopefully, we can catch this person very quickly."

After the Sheriff left, Mom came out and said, "Why don't you come into the kitchen and I will make you something to drink."

"Thanks Mom," Buck whispered.

The three went into the kitchen with heavy hearts, and a longing to see Blaze safe and sound. He had become an important part of their life.

Big Ed decided he needed to go to the barn, for there was much work to do, but mostly, because his spirit was heavy. Even though he knew a determined thief would get whatever they wanted, he couldn't help but think, *if only I had been more watchful, maybe this would not have happened.*

## CHAPTER 17

Sam got out of his truck, looking around at the unkempt yard and house, and began to be concerned about whether he had made the right decision about bringing the colt here. He hadn't seen his old friend for a few years, but knew that he would do just about anything for a few dollars. He had years of experience as a trainer of horses, but now only rarely did he work in that field. He had gotten out of the business full time, because people found him rough, and were concerned that he would abuse their valuable animals. Now he raised a few cows and horses, and with a little training on the side, he could survive. Sam knew that money was always an issue with Jerome.

Sam climbed the stairs to the porch and was about to knock when the door burst open, and a gruff voice said, "What do you want?"

"Greetings Jerome, thought I would stop and say howdy, on this *fine* day." Sam said, offering his hand for a friendly shake.

"Don't call me Jerome, if you don't want to get a black eye. I *hate* that name. You call me Jerry, but not Jerome. By the way, *who* are you and *what* do you want? Make it quick."

Pulling his hand back, after the rebuff, Sam replied. "Name's Sam, we used to be friends some years back. Spent some time together in the cattle business, and then some time in the county jail. You should remember, we had a lot of fun with those guards."

"Yeah, I remember. You always was a wise guy. Why're you here. I don't need no help."

"Got a job for you Jerry. Got a young horse in the trailer. I need to get some training on the animal before I sell him."

"Why'd you bring him to me? There are other trainers around, probably not as good as me, but more refined and upstanding." He bragged.

"Well, I didn't come by this horse in the *regular* way, and I knew you could do the job. Also, your place is hidden from the road and from prying eyes."

"Okay, so you *stol'* the horse. So, what would I get out of the deal?" Jerry retorted.

"How about 30 percent of the selling price. I would like to sell the animal to the circus that is coming through here in a few weeks, but if that doesn't happen then I might take him to Mexico. I saw this animal at the county fair and was impressed with his abilities, so I anticipate that we can get a higher price if he had a little more training."

"Let's have a look at this *super* horse," Jerry sarcastically muttered.

They went to the trailer and unloaded Blaze. The animal knew something was not right and threw his head back and let out a loud bellow and began to buck and kick. "Feisty critter," Jerry grumbled. "We will get *that* out of him purty dang quick."

Sam grabbed the bridle, and together they led Blaze to the barn, just beside the corral. After putting Blaze in the stall, Sam said, "Hey Jerry, when was the last time you cleaned this place up?"

"I only do it when it needs it." He retorted.

"Maybe it would be a good time to start. We don't want this horse to come down with something. At least not until we get rid of him." Sam chuckled.

**

Big Ed walked over to the refrigerator in the barn, pulled out a beer, sat down on an old stump he used as a stool, and closed his eyes. –He began to consider all the possibilities of what might have happened, and what might be the thief's desires for the horse.

He seriously doubted that the thief would want to keep the horse. His motive must be the money, and the potential of a big payday. How could they get the most money from a buyer for an untrained horse? A wild thought flashed through Big Ed's mind: *give the horse some professional training, thereby increasing its value.*

*Who would buy a trained or a partially trained horse, would the circus?* Big Ed paused when those words came into his thoughts. He immediately thought of Sam. *I can't believe we are back to Sam,* Big Ed thought. *It is hard to believe he would steal Blaze but it's beginning to look more and more like Sam is the culprit. It has to be Sam. He was here with his truck and horse trailer, and he asked about buying Blaze. I remember telling him that the horse was not for sale, at any price. He must have decided, 'If I can't buy it, I will steal it.'*

Big Ed walked into the kitchen where the others were sitting, and said, "I think I might have an idea." It was clear that what he was about to say caused him some deep concern. "Do you remember that friend of mine who came here a few weeks ago, and was admiring Blaze? He asked me if he was for sale and I told him no, not for *any* price. He also told me that he scouted and bought horses for the circus." Big Ed paused for a second and went on, "I am beginning to think that he might have something to do with this theft. I also believe that the horse will have to have more training, to make the most of the sale that I am *sure* Sam intends. I think the first place to start is to look for a trainer down south." Big Ed got a little louder and determined, saying, "I'm going to look up that scoundrel, old Sam. I am thinking he might come out of this with a couple of black eyes and a broken nose."

"Yeah!" they all cried out as one.

"Big Ed, you know that my dad is a trainer and Mr. Tanner is a farrier, you know, a guy who shoes horses. If you're right, I'll bet that between my dad and Mr. Tanner, we can find out where Blaze might be." Kate exclaimed.

# CHAPTER 18

Kate ran up to the front door of her house, shouting, "Dad! Dad, where are you? Mom, where's dad?" she cried out.

"He's out back with a customer." Mom replied.

"Did you know that Blaze has been stolen, and we don't know where he is?"

"Oh, I didn't know," mom replied as she put her hand over her mouth. The horrified look on her face was enough to bring tears to Kate's eyes. "Do you think your Father can help?" Mom asked.

"Big Ed said that he knew a guy who came to the ranch a few weeks ago and wanted to buy Blaze. He thinks that maybe he wanted Blaze for the circus, because he saw him at the fair. He thinks that maybe Blaze needs more training, so maybe some trainer has Blaze."

"Hold on Kate, I'll get your dad!"

**

"What's this all about Kate? Her dad anxiously ask. "You say that Blaze has been stolen?"

"Yes, he was taken sometime last night. When the Sheriff came out to the ranch, Buck had spotted some tracks that led to the road and then to a truck and a trailer. The Sheriff drove to the intersection and found the tracks that turned south. Big Ed thinks that he knows who would have done it and thinks this guy would need to train Blaze for a little longer so he could sell him to the circus. If the circus won't buy him, Big Ed thinks he will take Blaze to Mexico." She anxiously exclaimed, while she took a breath.

"Slow down Kate, how can I help?" Chuck Samuels asked skeptically.

"We thought maybe you or Mr. Tanner might know of somebody south of here who might be a trainer who could give Blaze some more training. This guy, Big Ed called Sam Peterson, might be friends with some trainer, and thinks he might have taken Blaze to his farm." Kate anxiously said.

"I know that there is a guy that used to train horses, who lives somewhere down toward Donley. I doubt he would do the job because he doesn't have a very good reputation. He didn't treat the horses very well and besides, his place was always dirty. He was always one step away from the law."

"Do you know what his name is and where he lives?" Kate excitedly asked.

"No, I can't remember his name, but Joe Tanner gets down into that area occasionally. I'll give him a call." Dad replied, while picking up the phone.

"Yes, I remember a character like that." Mr. Tanner offered. "As a matter of fact I have been to his place to shoe a couple of his horses. Strange fellow he is. Gruff and not very friendly. A rather ornery character. His horses don't seem to like him very much."

"Do you remember his name?" Chuck asked.

"Let's see if I can remember. About two hours south and then east for a couple of miles. I think I could find it if I tried but I don't think I can explain the turnoff."

"Do you remember his *name*?" Chuck impatiently ask again.

"Let's see, it seems that his first name is Jerome, I believe, although he might go by something else. I'll have to think about his last name."

"Do you think you could go down there and find out if Blaze *might* be there?" Chuck ask a little more patiently.

"What if I drove up to his place and told him I was looking for some work, and hopefully I will be able to spot the horse. If I can see him we can get the Sheriff down to his place to arrest him. We can get Blaze back and get one nasty criminal off the street." Mr. Tanner said, thinking as he talked.

"I believe his last name is Ketchum!" Mr. Tanner excitedly remembered.

# CHAPTER 19

Early the next morning, all were seated around the kitchen table, at the Tanner's house. Mrs. Tanner had fixed coffee and orange juice and had made some homemade donuts. They were in the midst of a planning session; trying to decide how to approach the difficult job of seeing if Blaze was at the Ketchum ranch. They knew they would have to get inside if they were to find out how he was being cared for. They all had questions and possible answers, but as of yet, no firm plan had developed.

"I could go see him and ask if there were any training positions around." Chuck Samuels offered. "The problem with that is he would probably run me off because he has no need of a trainer, and might suspect something." Chuck continued.

Big Ed thought for a while, silently thinking of all the different possibilities.

Kate stood up and excitedly said, "Why couldn't Mr. Tanner go there and ask if there are any horse shoeing jobs around. And while he's there maybe he could look around and see if Blaze might be there."

"I could do that," Mr. Tanner said. "And hope that he has the need of a farrier, and if so, I could do the job while I'm there. I could offer him a freebie of some sort. Maybe inspect some of his horse's shoes, or fix some harness, just to show him I would like his business. Most people like free stuff, and a grouchy old man is no different. He's probably as tight as an old rusty nail."

Mr. Tanner continued, "If I see Blaze I will leave as quickly as possible, and will call you so you can then call the Sheriff. It might take two or three hours for the Sheriff to get there. We can be waiting up by the highway in case Ketchum gets suspicious, and tries to run for it. He would need a horse trailer, and most of them are not fast enough when pulled behind an old truck."

The excitement around the table grew, because they were beginning to think that they had a reasonably good idea where Blaze might be. They were beginning to come up with a workable plan to rescue Blaze. They began the planning stages of when they should start, and how they would go about getting the Sheriff there.

"I believe we should call the Sheriff and tell him what we have planned." Chuck Samuels said.

"The problem with telling the Sheriff first, is he would probably tell us that we would need a search warrant, and no judge would give him one without some proof that Blaze is there. We *must* remember, we have no proof that he is there." Big Ed cautioned. He continued, "We are trusting on our belief that he is there. We must prove that he is there before the Sheriff will act."

"Okay, here is what we can do," exclaimed Mr. Tanner. "I will go to the ranch and attempt to prove that Blaze is there. I will then leave and call you, Big Ed, and you can then call the Sheriff. Hopefully, we can get everybody in place, and get Blaze back without any difficulty. We must understand that this is serious business, when a person is faced with a crime, they can become unpredictable."

"So, when do we start?" Buck excitedly asked. "I think we should start now."

"Not so fast," Big Ed said. "We need to take it one step at a time. Mr. Tanner, if you are agreeable can we start early tomorrow morning?"

Mr. Tanner nodded his head, and said, "Yes. If we gather here tomorrow morning at 6 o'clock, I believe we can do it. The rest of today we can get

91

ready. I will get my rig loaded and filled with gas and tools, while you guys get your truck and trailer ready to go. I will leave first, and you can follow a little later. Make sure your cell phones are fully charged, but don't forget that there might not be service in that part of the county. This could get tricky, but I think we can do it."

The rest of the day, they all worked to get ready for the rescue of Blaze. They each had their own thoughts about the little horse, and how much they were concerned about it.

Buck's mind returned to the time he had rescued Blaze from the wolf, while standing in the cold pond water.

Kate's thoughts were on the time they were training Blaze for the fair, and how much talent Blaze had.

Scotty recalled the time they were training Blaze, how he had run off. He recalled how Blaze had looked over the area where his mother had fought the wolf, and where his rescue had taken place.

They all loved Blaze, and were troubled that tomorrow might not work out.

Returning to their homes to spend the rest of the day and evening, they went to bed a little earlier than normal. All were anxious and concerned about tomorrow, and what awaited them. They slept fitfully throughout the night and at 5 am; the alarm clock aroused this sleepy trio. They jumped out of bed, none of them especially well-rested. Today was the day they hoped to be the day of rescue.

# CHAPTER 20

At 6 am sharp, all were gathered around the Winslow table, talking excitedly while passing each other dishes of eggs, pancakes and bacon. The anticipation was building, and giving way to a little worry that Blaze *might* not be there, but nobody was talking about it.

"I will go by myself, and the rest of you should go together in the large pickup." Mr. Tanner explained to the group, as he finished his last bite of bacon. "The big truck is large enough to seat everyone, and pull the trailer as well."

He looked around the table, and his eyes settled on Big Ed for a moment, "Big Ed is familiar with the vehicle so he will drive and Chuck, you will be the lookout and keep these youngsters in line," Mr. Tanner instructed with a slight nod towards Big Ed. "Remember, this is serious business and it could be dangerous, although I don't think it will come to that."

"Are all the cell phones charged?" Chuck Samuels asked.

"Yes!" they all answered at once, and surprised themselves with their volume and enthusiasm;

They were a team. A team with a mission - "Let's get going!" Buck shouted, the others echoed "Let's go!" as they were running towards the trucks.

They left about 6:30 and expected to be there about 8:30.

*I wonder what we can expect.* Mr. Tanner thought. He was driving ahead of the others, at a reasonable speed. *The only flaw in this matter is what if the Sheriff can't come as quickly as we hope. I guess we will have to wait. It is a two-hour drive, and a lot can happen in two hours.*

*

The turn was just up the highway, and Mr. Tanner slowed his work truck down. When he had made the turn onto the road he, steeled himself for what he had to do. He was a tough man, but was very concerned for all that was required for this investigation.

**

*Knock! Knock!* he banged on the door to the house. "*Who's* there and *what* do you want?" a grouchy voice from inside yelled. "Why am I getting all these people knocking on my door," He grumbled.

"Just wanted to give you my card and introduce myself to you."

"Well *who* are you and what do you want?" Ketchum retorted, while opening the door.

"I'm just trying to drum up some business in this area. I shoe horses, and fix broken harnesses. I have been known to do some blacksmith work on the ranches that I serve. Here's my card." he said in one breath, as he stretched out his hand giving the card to Ketchum.

"Well I don't have anything right now for you to do. So I guess your time is *just* wasted."

Mr. Tanner's heart sank and he knew he had to think of something fast, or this was not going to work. If he was going to get into the stable, he must think of something that would get this old codger's attention.

"I'll tell you what I'll do," Mr. Tanner said. "If you have any broken harness, or some minor saddle repair, I'll do it while I am here, and charge you nothing this time. I would like to have you for a permanent customer. I have a couple of other ranches in this area that I service, and I would like to add you to my list."

"Tempting," Ketchum said. "I do have a couple of harnesses that need some repair, and a saddle needing work. If you could do those, I just *might* use you in the future." He smiled to himself, thinking he was going to get something without having to pay for it. What an *idiot* this Tanner was. "Okay," he said, and stuck out his hand.

"You can call me Jerry, Jerry Ketchum."

"Okay Jerry, show me the way." They walked into the barn, and Ketchum took him directly to the tack room, grabbed a saddle and a couple of harnesses, and placed them on the workbench. "Have at it Tanner," he smirked. "I'll watch what you do and see if you are as good as you *think* you are."

Mr. Tanner began to inspect the harnesses, and knew he must get old Jerry out of the barn for a few minutes, so the way would be clear for him to inspect the stalls. His plan was to see if Blaze was there, but Ketchum planted himself, comfortably, on a stack of lumber in the corner, so he could watch Mr. Tanner do his work.

Finally, after about an hour, Mr. Tanner knew he was not going to be able to get Ketchum out of the barn, for even a short time, so he decided to take a more direct approach.

"Hey Jerry, are you still training horses." Mr. Tanner asked.

"Well, occasionally, I get a job now and then but not very often. I have a job going right now but it won't last long. A guy I used to know asked me to do a little work on this young horse, before taking it to Mexico."

"Sounds interesting," Mr. Tanner said. "Can I see this horse, and make sure it's okay for the trip."

"Sure, why not," Ketchum said. "He's just down this row of stalls."

As they approached one of the stall doors, Ketchum grabbed the sliding latch, pulled it back, and opened the door. Inside was a horse that Mr. Tanner recognized immediately. It was Blaze.

"That's a good looking horse you have there," Mr. Tanner said, trying not to betray his delight at having found Blaze. It appears to be healthy. I am sure its owner will be very happy with it."

"Yeah, that's why old Sam brought him here. He wants me to get him ready for his trip across the border. It will make the sale more profitable in Mexico."

*I have to get out of here,* Mr. Tanner thought. *Blaze is here, this place is a mess and the others are waiting for my answer.*

"Thanks for the look around Jerry. I guess I must be getting along. I have other stops to do today. If I can help in the future, just call. You have my card."

**

"He's there!" Mr. Tanner shouted to the others. "Call the Sheriff and get him rolling down here. Blaze is here, and he won't be here for very many days, so we must move fast."

"I just talked to the Sheriff, and he is on his way. It will take him about two hours to get here, even with his lights and siren. I guess we will have to just wait." Big Ed replied.

**

"Hey Sam, Jerry here. I just had a visit from a person that fixes harnesses and shoes horses. This

99

guy seemed okay, but he had a *keen* interest in seeing the horse you brought over here. After he left, I thought maybe I *might* have told him too much. You might want to pick him up for a few days, and hide him somewhere so if the Sheriff comes, we can keep him clueless." Ketchum growled.

*Jerry was never very smart,* Sam thought. He just might have ruined this whole thing. "Where was he from?" Sam asked.

"From up north I think, about two hours, why?"

"Because *that* is where I got this horse, and he just *might* have been a scout, or a person trying to find the horse. I'll be over there in about an hour. Get the horse ready, so when I pull the trailer in we can get him loaded in a hurry."

## CHAPTER 21

Sam Peterson was in a near state of panic. He quickly drove his truck and trailer toward the Ketchum ranch, knowing that he must hurry before the Sheriff got there. He turned down the road where the ranch was located, and spotted a truck with a horse trailer sitting by the road. He glanced at the truck and saw Big Ed, at the wheel, watching him. He knew that Big Ed couldn't arrest him, but he could stop him if he wished.

The thief turned into Jerome Ketchum's ranch, and rushed to the barn where they kept Blaze. They backed Blaze out of the stall in the old dilapidated barn, and took him to the trailer and began to load him.

"Come on Jerry, give me a hand. I just saw them down the road, probably waiting for the Sheriff." Sam anxiously and impatiently growled.

It took about five minutes for them to get Blaze into the trailer. Sam turned to Jerome and asked, "Is there another way out of here apart from going up the road toward the highway?"

"Yeah," replied Ketchum. "When you get down to the road turn right instead of left and go two miles, then turn south for five miles, and then right again and it will take you to the highway. It is a good road, a little bumpy in places, but it will get you to the highway. When you get to the highway you can then turn south again toward Mexico."

Sam, the thief, drove out of the driveway and turned right. He followed all the instructions, and about twenty minutes later, he reached the highway. The thief, the truck and trailer with Blaze, headed south toward Mexico.

**

Anxiously, Chuck looked at Big Ed and ask, "Do you think he will come back this way, or is there another way for him to go? I think he would have to come back this way by now, but there might be a back way out of here."

"I'll drive back to the Ketchum ranch and have a look, and see if I can find out where they are," volunteered Mr. Tanner. "If I see they have gone another way I will call you on your cell, providing I have a signal. If I don't get through I think you should get back on the highway and head toward the border. We are pretty sure that is where he's headed, so maybe we can head him off." Turning around, Mr. Tanner rushed down to the Ketchum ranch. Seeing nothing, he hurried back toward Big

Ed and the others. Mr. Tanner, in a puzzled manner, said. "I looked up the driveway and didn't see any vehicles. I think they must have gone out another way. We have lost time because the cell phones have no signal, so I think we should be heading for the highway, the faster the better."

\*\*

The thief looked in his rear view mirror and felt that he had made it without arousing the suspicions of the others. He knew it was only a matter of time before they would figure out what he was doing. He looked down at his speedometer and realized he was traveling a little fast for his rig, and decided to slow down just a bit, so he wouldn't arouse too much attention. Getting a ticket from the highway patrol would ruin his plans.

When he saw there was nothing behind him, he relaxed a little and starting thinking about getting into Mexico. *A good price for a good horse.* Sam started humming and thinking about his good fortune.

\*\*

Big Ed turned the truck south on the highway and accelerated to the speed limit. "Faster!" Buck yelled. "He is going to get away!"

Big Ed pushed the truck to its limit, and held on while searching ahead to see if there was any traffic. About five minutes later he spotted a truck and trailer, and excitedly pulled closer, ready to pass and then to stop this vehicle. As he got closer he realized it was not Sam's rig. Big Ed pulled closer, waiting for the traffic to clear, when Kate yelled "He's getting away, pass this slowpoke!"

Once again, the highway was clear and as they topped a rise in the road, they saw Sam Peterson with their horse, Blaze, in the distance.

"There he is, that rustler!" Scotty fumed. "Faster Big Ed, we can't let him get away!"

**

The sheriff pulled onto the highway and turned on his lights and siren and headed south at a high rate of speed. Things were starting to get hot and the border was closer to them than to him so he must hurry. With his cruiser going as fast as he dared, he called for backup from the highway patrol. The highway patrol couldn't respond immediately because they were working an accident in another part of the county. The sheriff knew he was on his own. *Faster!* He said to himself. *We must get there quickly or that dirty rotten thief will have that animal across the border, and he will be lost forever.*

# CHAPTER 22

Sam, the thief, fearfully looked in his rearview mirror, and knew that the owners of Blaze were behind him, and drawing closer. He pushed the truck to its limits and gained a little distance, hoping the truck would stay together. He knew the border was only a few more miles ahead and that meant he didn't have much time. The traffic was starting to pick up, and slower traffic began to hinder his mad dash. Sam was in no mood for safety, he just wanted to get across the border with his prize, and be done with that bunch following him, forever.

**

"That's him Big Ed, we're catching up with him." shouted Buck.

"Come on Big Ed!" shouted Scotty, "Pass this guy. He's only about two miles from the border, and if we lose him there, he's gone forever!"

Big Ed tried to pass but the slow driver in front wouldn't get out of the way. Finally a space opened up and pass they did, only to see that the thief was nowhere in sight.

"Maybe when we top that rise ahead we can see them. The border is just down below on the flat plain." Chuck anxiously whispered.

When they had topped the rise, they saw the truck pull up to the crossing and stop. There were two cars ahead of the thief as he pulled in line, and two cars behind. As one car was motioned forward by the agents, they knew there were just minutes to spare.

Big Ed knew he had to do something fast, or they were going to lose Blaze. He jumped out of the truck and shouted to Chuck Samuels. "Get the bolt cutters from the back and cut his lock, while I get to this guy, and convince him to give himself up!"

**

Sam, startled, looked back at Big Ed racing toward him, and knew he was as mad as a hornet. He had better do something fast. The border agent motioned him forward and stepped in front of his truck. Sam, the thief, knew he was cornered. He could not believe it when his side window shattered and Big Ed's fist came through the window, and grabbed the keys from the ignition.

Big Ed opened the door, dragged Sam the thief out, and threw him to the ground in one swift gesture. Sam did not see that coming.

**

Chuck Samuels retrieved the bolt cutters, and racing to the trailer attempted to cut the lock. It was a strong lock and the cutters were smaller than what was needed. After a couple of powerful tries, he was pleased with the sound of the lock snapping. He yanked the lock off and opened the doors to the trailer. He raced toward the front of the trailer, untied Blaze, and backed him out.

Kate was quick behind her dad, and took the reins from him, then gave the reins to Buck, as they all three happily got Blaze out of the trailer. They felt they needed to get Blaze away from the checkpoint.

"We should get him back as far away as we can so they can't say he is in Mexican territory!" exclaimed Buck.

**

The border agent was astonished at all the activity, and being unsure of what was going on, placed her hand on her gun, and ordered Big Ed to stop and explain what was happening.

"This man is a horse thief. He stole that horse from those three youngsters. We followed him here, and we are taking back what belongs to us."

Sam, the thief, puffed up and yelled, "He's a liar! I bought that horse fair and square." He took a breath, and added, "Fair. AND. Square!"

"Show me your receipt if you bought the horse." The agent ordered.

"I lost it on the drive down here." Sam angrily retorted.

They all stopped and turned when they heard a cruiser with its siren wailing, and lights flashing. The sheriff had arrived.

It did not take the sheriff long to sort it out with the border agent, and placed Sam Peterson, horse thief, under arrest. After placing handcuffs on the thief's wrists, the sheriff read him his Miranda rights. The Sheriff then roughly placed him in the back seat of his patrol car.

Buck, Kate and Scotty were standing back a few yards when the Sheriff arrested the thief. They hadn't noticed the little crowd that had gathered behind them. As they turned to walk towards Big Ed and Chuck, they heard an uproar of shouting and clapping, that made their hearts soar. It was only then that they knew their ordeal was officially over.

"Okay Blaze, bow to the people and tell them howdy." Buck instructed. Blaze dropped his head, half kneeled, and bowed to the people, amidst whistles and cheering.

Mr. Tanner rushed up and breathlessly said, "Whew, I almost didn't make it! Let me punch that thief in the nose. They all started laughing, and Blaze tossed his head as if to say "thanks."

# CHAPTER 23

Early the next spring, with warm spring days slowly approaching, the three, Buck, Kate and Scotty decided they would go for a ride on the north range. The prairie was coming alive with new shoots of prairie grass, just beginning to turn green. The day was cool, the sun was shining, and their spirits were high.

The winter had been long, and cold for months. Blaze had a nice warm barn, which they locked every night. He was back and acted as if nothing had happened.

"Turn Blaze out and let's follow him, and have some fun chasing him." Kate laughed.

They turned Blaze loose and immediately Blaze, with mane and tail flying, started running like the wind, back toward the east.

"Where's he going?" shouted Buck. "Let's follow and see where he goes."

When they finally caught up to Blaze, he had come to a stop at the fence separating the O'Donnell Ranch and the Winslow ranch.

"Look," exclaimed Kate. "There's Princess, Jimmy O'Donnell's filly. "And will you look at Blaze."

"What is he standing so close to her for?" Asked a confused Scotty.

They had a laugh at Scotty, and Kate exclaimed,

"Did you see that Buck? Blaze turned and winked at me."

"Horses don't *wink* Kate," Scotty scolded. "Just look at him nuzzling up to the black Princess."

Kate shouted again, "Look, he just winked at me again."

********

## About the Author

Mr. L. Wayne has been a small business man all of his adult life, and when he retired a few years ago he decided to keep busy by putting into print some of his thoughts and ideas. His first three books were titled, "The Purpose of Human Existence," "The Practical God," and "God's Master Plan." After the publishing of these three important books, he decided to write a fictional account of three teenagers and their adventures during the summer of their 15$^{th}$ year.

"Adventures of Blaze - the Rescue" is the first in what will be a 3 part series. The next is tentatively titled "Adventures with Blaze – The camping Trip.

He and his wife "Sharon" live in Wichita, Ks

Made in the USA
Columbia, SC
28 September 2017